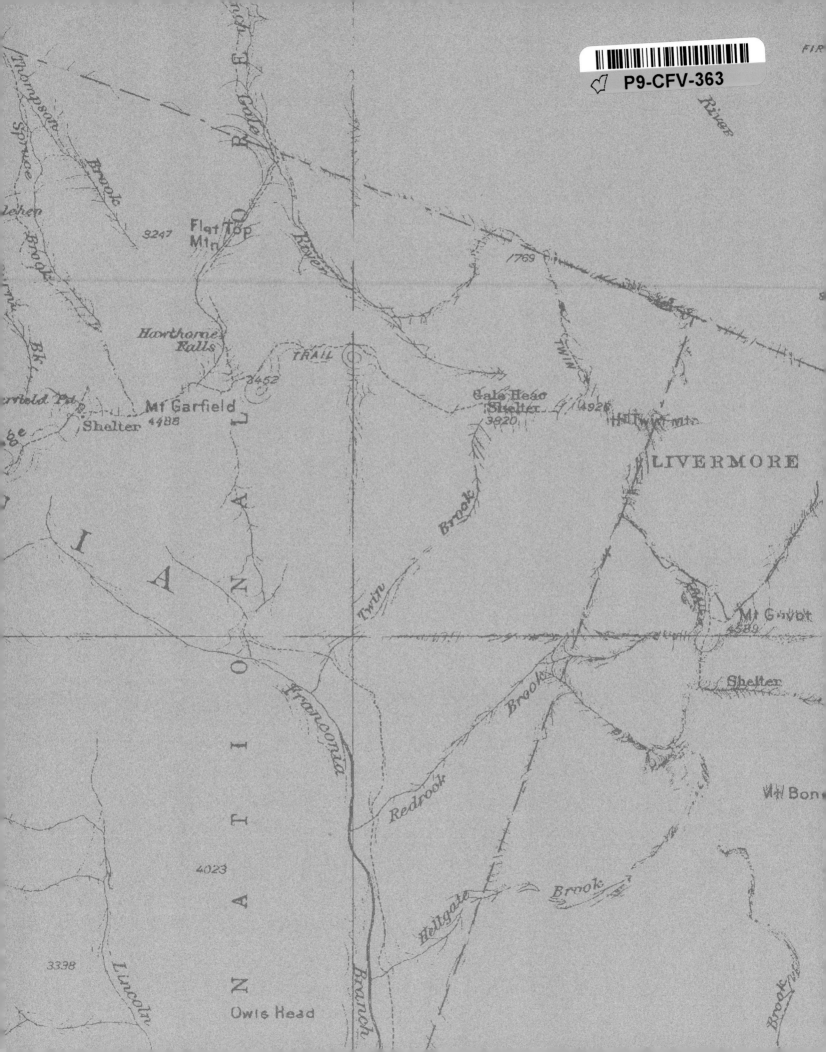

The Legend of the Old Man of the Mountain

By Denise Ortakales
Illustrated By Robert Crawford

To my brothers, David and Mark,
with whom I remember many picnics under the Old Man's gaze

—*Denise*

I would like to dedicate this book to my parents, Claire and Richard
Crawford, whose love and support have helped me all through my life.

—*Robert*

I would like to thank the Institute for American Indian Studies in
Washington, CT for their outstanding exhibits and the help they provided
me in my research and also the Mashantucket Pequot museum and website.
I would also be pleased to acknowledge the help of Sarah Baldwin and
Andrew Wanat for their time and patience as models.   —*R.C.*

Sleeping Bear Press
310 North Main Street, Suite 300
Chelsea, MI 48118
www.sleepingbearpress.com

© 2004 Thomson Gale, a part of the Thomson Corporation.

Thomson, Star Logo and Sleeping Bear Press are trademarks
and Gale is a registered trademark used herein under license.

Printed and bound in Canada.

10 9 8 7 6 5 4 3 2

Library of Congress Cataloging-in-Publication Data

Ortakales, Denise.
The legend of the old man of the mountain / written by Denise Ortakales ;
illustrated by Robert Crawford.
p. cm.
ISBN 1-58536-236-0
1. Indians of North America—New Hampshire—Folklore. 2. Legends— New Hampshire.
3. Old Man of the Mountain (N.H.)—Folklore. I. Crawford, Robert, 1953- ill. II. Title.
E78.N54O78 2004
398.2'089'97—dc22   2004009801

About The Old Man of the Mountain

Many yarns and tall tales have been spun about the Old Man of the Mountain as he stood witness to the comings and goings of the people in his valley. Some legends were written down and others recounted around the campfire. I chose to retell one that reflected the characteristics of the Granite State—strength, loyalty, determination, endurance, and faith.

Formed by ice sheets that covered North America millions of years ago, the Old Man of the Mountain was a group of five ledges on the face of Profile, or Cannon Mountain, that when viewed from a particular angle gave the appearance of a man's face. Made from Conway Granite, the Old Man measured 40 feet tall, 25 feet wide, and stood 1,200 feet off the ground.

The first European men to discover the profile observed it in 1805, and since then millions have come to Franconia Notch, New Hampshire, to catch a glimpse of the Old Man. Nathaniel Hawthorne wrote a story about the Old Man in 1850 called *The Legend of the Great Stone Face.*

In 1916 it was decided to fortify the ledges with supporting cables because many feared that the profile was in danger of tumbling. He became New Hampshire's state symbol in 1945 and appears on its license plates and road signs, two U.S. postage stamps, and is featured on New Hampshire's state quarter.

Sadly in the early morning hours of May 3, 2003, the Old Man of the Mountain tumbled to the ground. It is generally thought that the elements—the harsh New Hampshire winters and the repeated freezing and thawing of water in the cracks of the granite—brought the Old Man down. Although the Old Man of the Mountain is gone, he will never be forgotten. Some people say that with his falling, the Old Man's spirit has been released and that he is now free.

—Denise Ortakales

There was a time when others inhabited this land. They tilled the soil, trod the paths, and fished the streams. They lived in a village alongside the river, in the shadow of the great White Mountains. They were proud and had a great respect for the fertile land. They were called the Pemigewasset, after the name of their great and well-respected Sagamore (chief).

Chief Pemigewasset proved to be a fearless opponent against the Mohawk, a tribe from the west. The Pemigewasset had fought the Mohawk many times. However, this battle was not about only warring tribes. This battle included the meeting of Pemigewasset and the enchanting Minerwa, daughter of the Mohawk's chief. She too was captivated by Pemigewasset's good looks, agility, and skill as a warrior. So when her tribe returned home, she chose to stay with Pemigewasset, to be his wife. For the first time in many years there was peace between their tribes because of the love they shared.

Pemigewasset's life with Minerwa was a happy union. They spent many an hour walking hand-in-hand throughout the forest, reveling in the splendor that surrounded them. Minerwa never tired of hearing Pemigewasset's bird calls, or the hunting stories he would amuse her with. For his part, Pemigewasset was charmed by Minerwa's knowledge of herbs and plant lore, and the way she would hum while they walked.

One day during the planting season Minerwa's brother arrived with a message from her father. "*Kwai, Nidokan.* Hello, my brother. It is good to see you! What brings you here?" asked Minerwa as she ran to hug him.

"Yes, little Minerwa, it has been too many years," he exclaimed. "I can see that you have flourished here."

She laughed. "Yes I have, big brother. But your eyes are deceiving you for I am not so little any more!" Her laughter faded as she noticed a sadness in his eyes. "Tell me, why have you come?"

Taking her hands into his, he said, "It is our father. He is dying and would like to see you again."

With tears spilling from her, Minerwa ran to find the comfort of Pemigewasset's arms. "Tell me what is wrong," he pleaded, gently stroking her hair.

"Husband, my father will be going to the Great Spirit Manitou soon and he wants to look upon my face one last time," a tearful Minerwa wept.

The great warrior looked sorrowfully at his wife. He knew she must go. It was his duty to accompany her lest he offend the other tribe, yet his foot, long ago injured in battle, prevented him from attempting the long and arduous journey. "How he must have missed you all these years. If seeing you one last time will allow him to rest peacefully, then he shall have his wish. It would be wrong of me to deny him such a pleasure. In my stead I shall send several of my warriors to guide and guard you until you return to my side."

In the days following, Minerwa prepared for her long trip. Furs, baskets, and other gifts were collected to present to the Mohawks to show gratitude for the years of peace that had reigned over their land. She looked forward to seeing her family again but was reluctant to leave her beloved husband behind. Finally, the gifts and food for the travelers were carefully packed.

Pemigewasset chose three of his best men to escort Minerwa. First he chose the best hunter of the tribe to make sure they would not want for food; second he chose the fiercest warrior who would protect Minerwa from any harm; and third he chose the tribe's best guide to make sure Minerwa didn't lose her way back home.

"*Adio. Olibamkanni*, Good-bye, have a good trip!" called out the villagers as the group of travelers departed on their long journey.

Pemigewasset accompanied them for as long as he was able. "I shall not rest until you return," sighed Pemigewasset.

"I'll return," promised Minerwa as she gave her husband a final embrace.

The Sagamore set up camp on a hill with several braves, while Minerwa and her guardians traveled onward. From the camp, Pemigewasset sent smoke signals to Minerwa every sunset, and every sunset she would send a message back, until they were so far apart they could no longer see the smoke rising. Only then, with a heavy heart, did Pemigewasset return to his village alongside the river to await Minerwa's homecoming, when the Harvest Moon would show itself in the sky.

On Pemigewasset's return he tended
the tobacco crop and fished in the cool
waters of the river. He even helped the
children search for nuts and berries.
He tried not to think of Minerwa.

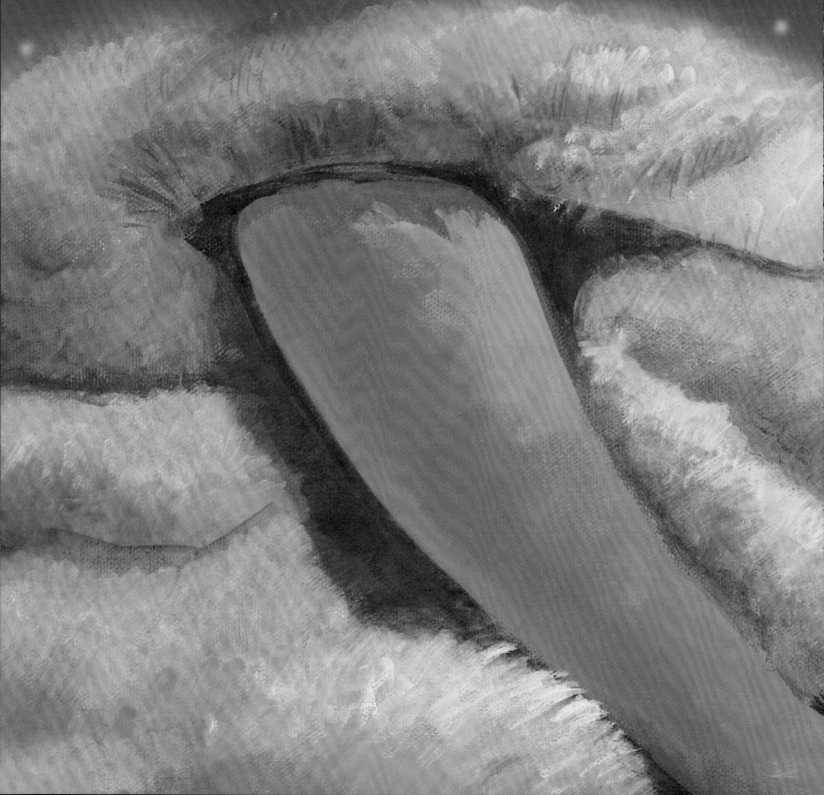

But it was during the long nights that he missed her the most, tossing and turning until she finally came to him in his dreams, speaking to him of her love, soothing his aching heart with her voice. "*Oligawi. Olegwasi.* Sleep well, dream well," she would whisper until he fell into a tranquil slumber. And so it was he passed the long summer awaiting Minerwa's return.

At the agreed-upon time, when the Huntsman in the sky slew the celestial Great Bear, the spilling blood staining the leaves scarlet, Pemigewasset and his braves climbed the highest cliff to await her return.

Every sunset he would send smoke signals, but they went unanswered. Days turned into weeks. The old moon had waned and the Hunter's Moon had now arisen, but there was still no sign of Minerwa.

Winter was drawing closer. As the weather worsened, so did Pemigewasset's health. Tired from his daily vigil, the Sagamore was sick with worry, yet he could not leave. "Construct a shelter and gather some food and firewood. I shall await Minerwa's return alone," instructed Pemigewasset.

"Great Pemigewasset, it is true that you are fierce and brave, but even the fiercest of warriors would have difficulty surviving up on this cliff alone when the snow flies," replied a reluctant brave.

"Your concern for me is honorable but there is nothing you can say that will deter me. I cannot go back on my word to Minerwa." They desperately tried to persuade him to return with them, but in the end they obeyed their ailing chief. They provided for him the best they could.

A sturdy shelter was built and it was filled with as much dry firewood and food as they could gather. After leaving their thick, warm skins for him, they sadly bid *adio* to Pemigewasset and descended the cliff, knowing what the harsh winter would bring.

Rising with the sun, Pemigewasset waited each day at the edge of the cliff overlooking the valley, hoping for that glimpse of Minerwa that would make his spirit soar. He prayed to Manitou to guide each of her footsteps until she was safely home.

There he stayed until darkness overcame him, only to retreat to his shelter where slumber awaited him.

He continued his search for his beautiful Minerwa in his dreams where he was not deterred by his crippled foot. He looked behind every tree and under every rock, investigated every sound and examined every broken twig, every footprint. He searched and searched until he could search no more.

The winter passed and, after the sap in the maple trees started to flow, a party of braves anxiously returned to the cliff. It was an early spring and most of the snow had melted. They were relieved to see the shelter was still standing but when they entered, their worst fears had come true. During the winter the Great Spirit had taken their chief, leaving only his lifeless body.

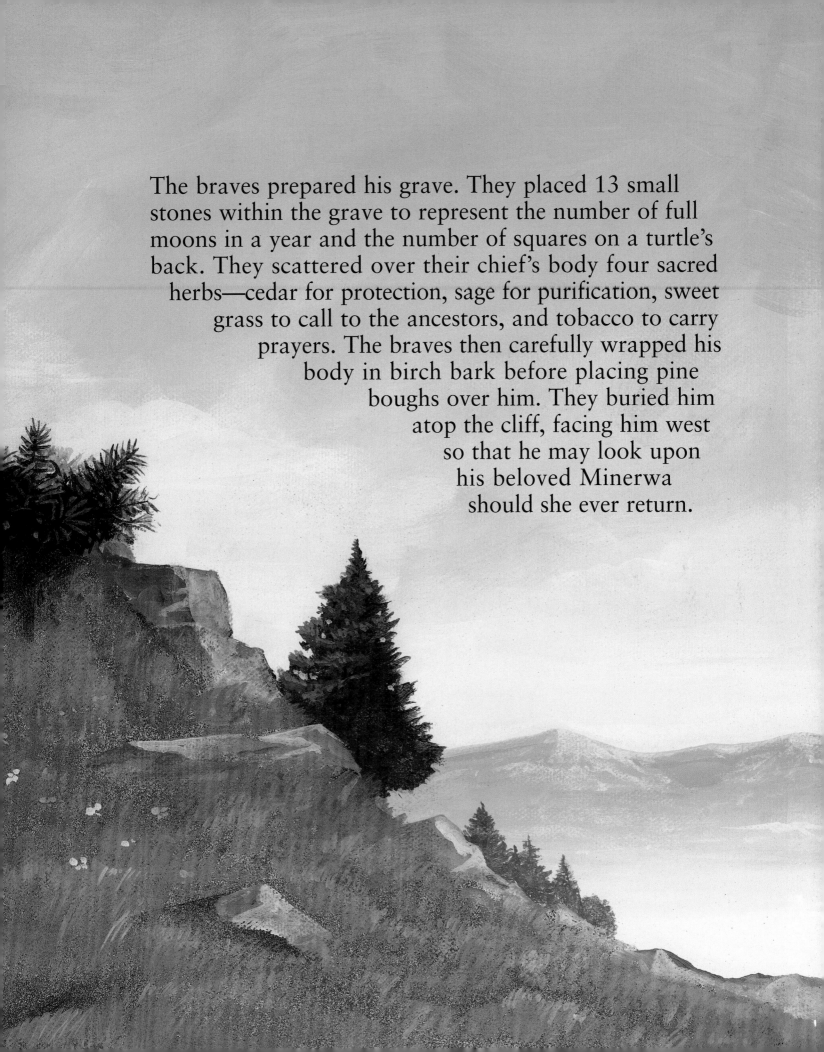

The braves prepared his grave. They placed 13 small stones within the grave to represent the number of full moons in a year and the number of squares on a turtle's back. They scattered over their chief's body four sacred herbs—cedar for protection, sage for purification, sweet grass to call to the ancestors, and tobacco to carry prayers. The braves then carefully wrapped his body in birch bark before placing pine boughs over him. They buried him atop the cliff, facing him west so that he may look upon his beloved Minerwa should she ever return.

Again the braves bid farewell to Pemigewasset and descended the cliff. Turning to take one last look, the braves were amazed by what they saw. The profile of Pemigewasset had been immortalized by the Great Spirit on the face of the cliff. The braves hurried back to their village alongside the river in the valley to tell the others.

Soon, all people came to see their revered leader on the mountainside. They came to see the place where he waited silently and eternally for the one dearest to his heart. They admired his devotion and, out of respect, left him gifts and offerings.

They honored their chief by calling the river that runs next to the cliff and into the valley, the Pemigewasset River. For many years the Great Stone Face looked out over the river that bore his name and the valley below where his people lived.

Denise Ortakales

Denise Ortakales graduated from the Art Institute of Boston, where she studied illustration and children's literature. Having grown up in the shadow of the Old Man, it was natural for her to write about it as a school assignment. Years later, when the granite formation fell, she knew it was time to share that story with others. This is her first book as an author. As an artist she has illustrated several picture books, including *Carrot in My Pocket* by Kitson Flynn, and *Good Morning, Garden* by Barbara Brenner, both done in her unique sculpted paper style. A lifelong resident of the Lakes Region of New Hampshire, she lives there with her husband and two sons. You can learn more about Denise at her website: deniseortakales.com.

Robert Crawford

Robert Crawford graduated with a BFA from Rhode Island School of Design. His paintings have appeared on the cover of major magazines such as *Fortune*, *Business Week*, *The Atlantic*, and *U.S. News and World Report* as well as book covers for best-selling books.

Robert's work has won numerous awards from the Society of Illustrators, *Communication Arts*, *Graphis*, and *Print*. His paintings have been included in group shows in New York, Japan, and Germany and he participated in the United Nation's sponsored show on the environment in New York City. Robert's studio is located in northwest Connecticut. Please visit Robert's website for more information: www.rcrawford.com.

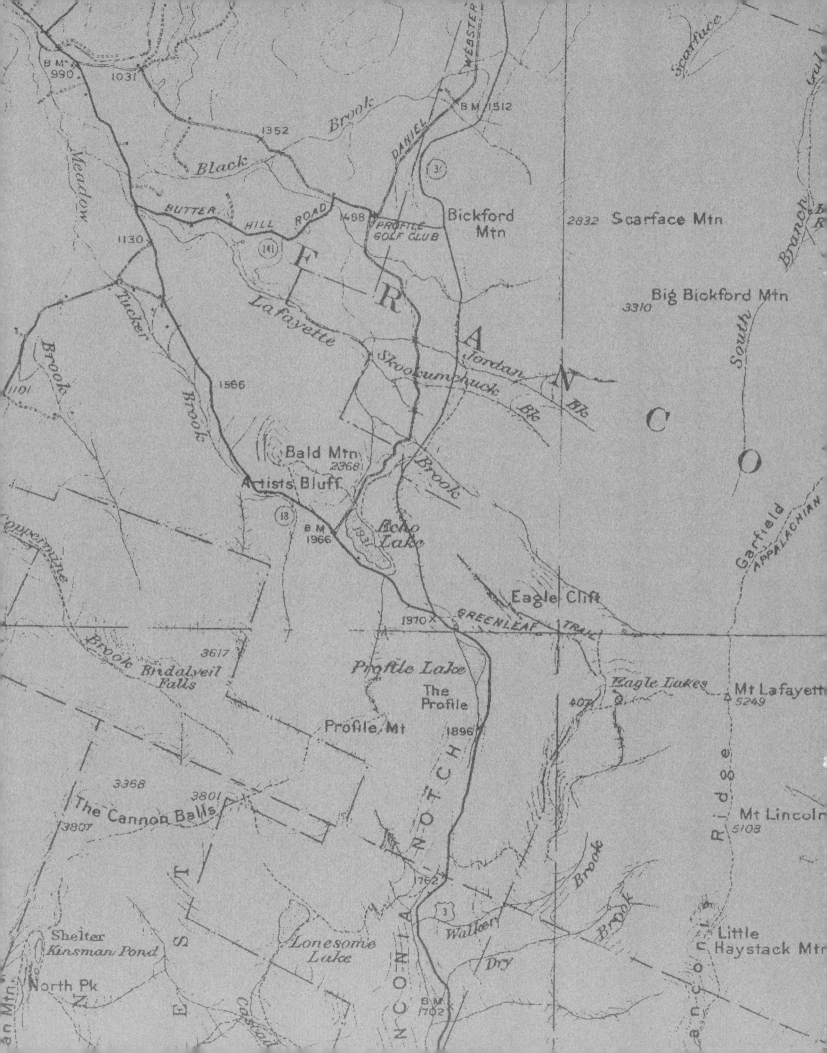